www.raintreepublishers.co.uk
Visit our website to find out
more information about
Raintree books.

To order:
☎ Phone 0845 6044371
▤ Fax +44 (0) 1865 312263
✉ Email myorders@raintreepublishers.co.uk

Customers from outside the UK please telephone +44 1865 312262

Raintree is an imprint of Capstone Global Library Limited,
a company incorporated in England and Wales having its
registered office at 7 Pilgrim Street, London, EC4V 6LB
– Registered company number: 6695582

First published by Stone Arch Books in 2010
First published in the United Kingdom in hardback and paperback in 2010
The moral rights of the proprietor have been asserted.

Art Director: Bob Lentz
Designer: Brann Garvey
Production Specialist: Michelle Biedschied
Editor: Vaarunika Dharmapala
Originated by Capstone Global Library Ltd
Printed and bound in China by Leo Paper Products Ltd

ISBN 978 1 406217 92 6 (hardback)
14 13 12 11 10
10 9 8 7 6 5 4 3 2 1

ISBN 978 1 406218 00 8 (paperback)
14 13 12 11
10 9 8 7 6 5 4 3 2

British Library Cataloguing in Publication Data
A full catalogue record for this book is available from the British Library.

CONTENTS

CHAPTER 1

BATMAN'S BUSY WEEK

BEEP! BEEP! BEEP!

The quiet Gotham City night had been broken by the loud ringing of a burglar alarm at Hawke's Jewellery Shop. Nearby, another alarm began to blare at Byrd's Stamps. A moment later, a third alarm joined the night chorus at Aves Art Museum.

The sleek, dark Batmobile screeched to a stop on 27th Street. Batman jumped out of the car and raced inside Byrd's Stamps.

Moments later, five police cars with flashing red lights zoomed down the street. Then, a squad of police officers ran to the dark gallery.

The man watching from a rooftop opposite Byrd's Stamps did not seem to care that the pouring rain dropped off the brim of his bright green bowler hat. He waited patiently, silent and still. Minutes later, the policemen and Batman came out of the gallery leading the Penguin away in handcuffs.

"I warned the Penguin that Batman would work out his scheme," the man said to himself. "But when is a warning like a group of cows in a field? Only when it's *heard*."

"That's funny!" squeaked an excited voice behind him.

"Who's there?" gasped the man in the green hat. He whirled around in surprise towards the voice.

No one was there! In front of him was only the empty roof and falling rain.

"No, no, up here!" said the voice.

The Riddler looked up and gasped again. He raised his question-mark shaped cane and shook it. "What are you supposed to be?" he asked.

"You're the Riddler. You work it out!" said the little man, giggling above him in mid-air. He had a round tummy, a merry smile, and a jolly twinkle in his eyes. He wore a loose-fitting, poorly made Batman costume. It had a lopsided bat-symbol stitched on the chest, and one bent bat-ear.

The Riddler said nothing. All his life, Edward Nigma had loved riddles. So, when he became a criminal, he took the name of the Riddler. He used crazy riddles and puzzles to tease Batman about his upcoming crimes. Even so, he couldn't explain this imp in a Batman costume.

"Oh, boy! I stumped the Riddler!" the little man squealed in delight. "I'm Bat-Mite, from another dimension. We watch what happens on Earth constantly. That's how I learned about Batman and became his greatest fan. Sometimes, I like to visit and help him fight crime."

Bat-Mite lowered himself to eye-level with the Riddler. "Batman yells a lot and pretends to hate it when I show up, but I know that deep down he's really very happy to see me," he whispered.

"Er . . . yes," said the Riddler, struck with a sudden idea. "We all love Batman! We know how much fun he has solving mysteries and figuring out crimes, so we wanted to give him a real challenge. It's kind of like a game. Why, he's having so much fun, he's been playing with us all week!"

The Riddler sighed and looked down at the street as the police car carried the crooked bird to jail. "Now he's caught the Penguin," said the Riddler. "I suppose it's up to me to come up with a really great mystery for him – all by myself."

"Oh, let me help, Riddler! Please, please, please!" Bat-Mite cried in excitement.

"What a wonderful idea," said the Riddler with a sly grin.

"You can help me make . . . a big game!" the Riddler said. "We'll make Batman the happiest Caped Crusader on Earth."

"Oooh," said Bat-Mite with a huge smile. "Yes, let's do that!"

* * *

As dawn lit the streets of Gotham City, the Batmobile returned to the Batcave. The great cavern was hidden beneath Wayne Manor. It was the home of billionaire Bruce Wayne, Batman's secret identity.

Bruce had discovered the cave, and the countless bats that lived there, when he was just a boy. Later, after his parents had been killed by a thief, he became Batman to protect other innocent people from criminals.

It was then that Batman had built the underground cavern. It had the world's fastest computers and the most modern equipment to help with his war against crime.

"Good morning, Master Bruce," said Alfred Pennyworth.

Alfred was a tall, thin man with a little moustache. He had been the butler of Bruce's parents. After their deaths, Alfred had raised the young orphan himself. Whether he was acting as Bruce Wayne or Batman, the billionaire crime fighter knew he could always rely on Alfred.

"Hello, Alfred," Batman said in a tired voice. He took the glass of orange juice his butler held out to him and quickly drank it down.

"Thank you," said Batman.

"You sound exhausted, sir," said Alfred.

"I am," Batman admitted. He pulled the cowl from his face and rubbed his eyes. "I haven't had much sleep since those ten villains escaped from Arkham Asylum."

"With the Penguin under arrest, the Riddler is the only one who is still free," Alfred said. "You need some sleep, Master Bruce."

"I'll sleep," said Bruce Wayne, "as soon as the Riddler is back behind bars."

CHAPTER 2

HOTEL HOLD-UP

After taking a shower and eating the big breakfast Alfred made for him, Bruce Wayne put on a clean Batman costume. He leaped into the Batmobile and fired up the engine. **BRROOOMMM!** Then he drove away in the Batmobile to continue his search for the Riddler.

The villain liked to tease and confuse Batman by leaving clues to his crimes in the form of riddles. The Riddler might outsmart him at first, but the Dark Knight always won in the end.

It had been many days since the Riddler had committed one of his puzzling crimes. Batman was sure that whatever the Riddler was planning next, it would be big.

BZZT! Suddenly, the private radio link with Gotham City's Police Commissioner James Gordon sounded.

Batman tapped a button and said, "Yes, Commissioner?"

"It's what you've been waiting for," said Commissioner Gordon. "A riddle from the Riddler! It says, 'What comes once in a minute, twice in a moment, but never in one thousand years?'"

"That's an easy one," Batman said. "The answer is the letter 'M'. Maybe that's a clue pointing to the new Millennium Hotel?"

"Could be," said the commissioner. "The giant, lighted 'M' on its roof is visible throughout the city," Gordon said.

"There's also a collection of rare Chinese puzzle dolls on display in the hotel's lobby," Batman added. "It's just the sort of prize the Riddler would want."

*   *   *

A porter in a bright green uniform entered the Millennium Hotel lobby. He pushed a trolley piled with suitcases, bags, and trunks. The great stack of luggage was so tall that it hid the porter's face.

"Excuse me," he called out. "Coming through! Excuse me!"

He was breathing hard as he pushed the heavy trolley. He rolled it closer to the display case in the centre of the lobby.

The porter moved past a large marble fountain. It sprayed a beautiful dome of water under the coloured lights. His eyes stayed on the display case.

A security guard stood by the case. It held ten dolls of ten ancient Chinese emperors. The dolls were more than a thousand years old. Each was about sixty centimetres tall and made of solid gold. Priceless jewels and gems decorated them.

Nine of the beautiful, glittering dolls were standing upright in the case. The last was in pieces to show that these works of art were also complex puzzles.

As he eyed the priceless dolls, the porter stumbled and tripped. As he fell, he lost his grip on the trolley.

"Whoops!" he shouted.

THUD! The trolley slammed against the display case.

"Hey, are you okay?" asked the security guard. He offered a hand to help the porter back to his feet. The porter grabbed the guard's hand.

"When is a stumble like a relaxing ride through the country?" asked the porter.

"What?" said the startled guard.

"When it's a just little trip!" said the porter, who began to giggle loudly.

With that, he yanked the guard to the ground. Suddenly, the huge pile of luggage on the trolley popped open like a blossoming flower. Hidden inside were two men. One grabbed the security guard. The other held a sledgehammer.

"Hit it, boys," said the Riddler.

The thug readied the sledgehammer, preparing to smash the display case.

"Don't even think about it," growled a voice from above.

The Riddler looked up and grinned.

"Batman!" he cried out, happily. "I thought you'd never get here!"

Batman leaped from the small balcony overlooking the lobby, swinging on a Batrope.

Just as Batman swung over the middle of the room, the great marble fountain erupted in an explosion of water from below. Batman gasped as the wall of cold water slammed into him. His fingers slipped from the rope, and he smashed into the fountain. KRASSSHHH!

The Caped Crusader struggled to his feet in the cold water of the slippery fountain.

POOF! Batman looked up. The Riddler and his men had vanished, along with the Chinese puzzle dolls.

"How did the Riddler do that?" Batman said aloud.

Batman thought he heard somebody giggling high above him. When he looked up, no one was there.

CHAPTER 3

THE RIDDLE OF THE RIDDLER

"No one saw the Riddler and his men escape with the puzzle dolls?" Batman asked. "How is that possible?"

The commissioner frowned. "Witnesses said there were a lot of people running around and yelling after you fell into the fountain. The Riddler probably slipped away in the confusion," Gordon said. "It's not like they magically disappeared or anything."

"I suppose not," said Batman, rubbing his chin.

Suddenly, a policeman raced up to Gordon and Batman.

"Sir," the officer said, handing the note to the commissioner. "We've just found this on the seat of our patrol car!"

He held a piece of green paper in his hand. It was decorated with a large black question mark.

"Did you see anybody near your car?" Gordon asked the officer.

"No, sir," he said, shaking his head. "One second, there was nothing. Then, like magic, the note appeared!"

Gordon read the note out loud. "'When one does not know what it is, then it is something. When one knows what it is, then it is nothing.'"

"A riddle!" said Batman.

Commissioner Gordon tilted his head at Batman in surprise. "Well, yes, of course it's a riddle," he said.

"No, the *answer* to the riddle is 'a riddle,'" said Batman.

"I don't get it," said the policeman.

"It's simple. A riddle becomes nothing after you solve it," Batman explained. "But what is the Riddler planning?"

*   *   *

"Did I do a good job, Riddler?" Bat-Mite asked, back at the Riddler's hideout.

The Riddler turned in his seat and smiled his best smile at the happy, giggling imp. "You did, little guy," he said. "Your magic got us – and those statues – out of that hotel without anybody seeing a thing."

"Don't forget the clue I put in that policeman's car!" said Bat-Mite. "Oh boy, can you imagine how much fun Batman's going to have trying to solve that riddle?"

"I can, pal!" said the Riddler with a chuckle. "I really can!"

*   *   *

A set of great stone steps led up to the entrance of the Gotham City Museum of Art. Every day, visitors came from all over to view the wonderful treasures inside.

Today, there was a painting called "Funny Money" by artist Roger Marshall on display. People came to view it, along with many other works of art.

One of those other treasures was a sculpture called "A Riddle" by the famous Gotham City artist Jerrold Robinson.

The sculpture was a life-sized, heavy steel statue of a man sitting with his chin resting on his fist. In his other hand, he held a large question mark. The figure had a confused look on his face. The statue sat alone in the gallery, under a skylight that filled the room with bright moonlight.

A helicopter flew down from the sky and hovered over the museum skylight for a moment. Then, suddenly, it dropped a heavy object attached to a rope. It struck the skylight, smashing the glass. **CRASH!!**

The object was a magnet! There were screams of fear as people ran out of the room. The magnet swung back and forth until it stuck to the steel statue. **CLANK!**

Batman raced into the room just as the helicopter started to lift the statue upwards.

"That's staying here, Riddler!" Batman shouted. With a mighty leap, the Dark Knight grabbed on to the statue. Then he began to pull himself up the rope.

The Riddler leaned out of the helicopter, waving and shouting. "Hey, Bats! I have a riddle for you!" he yelled. "When should you worry about having a good winter?"

The comedic criminal produced a pair of giant scissors from inside the helicopter. He opened the scissors and prepared to slice the rope in half.

"When it follows a bad fall!" the Riddler cackled as he cut the rope. *SNAP!*

With a shout of surprise, Batman and the statue began to fall towards the museum floor.

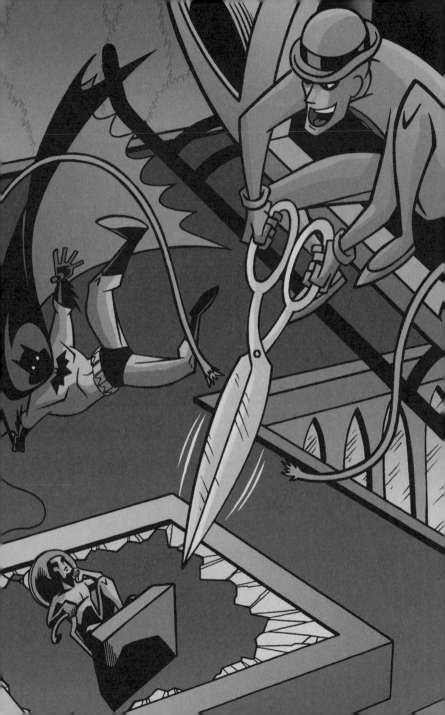

CHAPTER 4

THE BAT-MITE'S SURPRISE

As the Dark Knight fell, he reached into his Utility Belt for his grapnel gun.

 The grapnel latched into the ceiling beside the broken skylight. With a jerk, Batman swung safely to the floor.

The steel statue hit the floor – and shattered into a thousand pieces!

"Steel doesn't shatter!" said Batman in surprise. He examined a piece. "It's not steel . . . it's plaster!"

"That's impossible," Batman said to himself. "I saw the Riddler's magnet cling to the statue."

A piece of green paper poked out of the pile of broken pieces. Another clue!

Batman read the clue out loud. "'He who has it doesn't tell it. He who takes it doesn't know it. He who knows it doesn't want it. What is it?'"

The Dark Knight crumpled the green paper in his fist. "Hmm," he said softly to himself. "What is something that you wouldn't want if you knew what it was?"

"Of course!" Batman said. "The answer has to be counterfeit money!"

Moments later, Batman was back in the Batmobile speaking to Commissioner Gordon on the radio.

"The Riddler left a clue about counterfeit money," said the Dark Knight.

"Fake money? Hmm . . ." said the commissioner's voice. "You know, we took £100 million in counterfeit money from forgers a few days ago. We've been holding it here at police headquarters."

Gordon paused for a moment. "In fact," he said, "an armoured car is taking it to the rubbish dump right now! It left here just ten minutes ago!"

"That's it!" said Batman. "The Riddler plans to steal that funny money at the dump. I'll meet you there, Commissioner."

"We'll be ready for him," Gordon said.

"I've got you now, Riddler," Batman said to himself. "And none of your tricks will protect you this time."

*　　*　　*

"All units near Gotham City dump," crackled the police radio. "Commissioner Gordon has ordered all units to surround the rubbish dump and be on the lookout for an armoured car."

CLICK! The Riddler turned off the radio with a flick of his wrist. "Perfect!" said the criminal king of clues.

"Why?" asked Bat-Mite, his eyes wide.

"Because of you, my little friend!" said the Riddler, as he did a happy dance.

"Thanks to your magical powers, both the police and Batman are clueless, even after I've given them a clue!" Riddler said.

"I bet Batman's having so much fun!" Bat-Mite squealed in excitement.

"When is a bet not a bet?" said Riddler.

"I give up," Bat-Mite said. "When?"

"When it's a sure thing!" snorted the Riddler.

"Yay!" cheered Bat-Mite. "Um, what's a 'sure thing,' Riddler?"

"It's when something is too easy," said the Riddler. "With your help, tricking Batman is easier than stealing sweets from a baby."

"Oh, it is, is it?" the Bat-Mite said to himself.

Bat-Mite turned his head so the Riddler would not see the mischievous twinkle in his eyes. He giggled quietly to himself, trying as hard as he could to not let the Riddler hear him.

*   *   *

The sleek black Batmobile sped carefully through the Gotham City traffic. Behind the wheel, Batman knew he had no time to waste. If he was correct, the Riddler would soon grab his loot and then disappear.

"Are you in position, Commissioner?" Batman asked over the police radio.

"We have the rubbish dump surrounded," said Gordon. "We're ready!"

"I'll be there shortly," said Batman. He turned off the radio and smiled.

*   *   *

"Did you hear what Batman said, Bat-Mite?" said the Riddler, pointing to his police radio. "He's going to be at the rubbish dump in a few minutes!"

Bat-Mite clasped his hands over his mouth to stop his nervous giggling. "Shouldn't we get started, Riddler?" he asked.

"Yes, we should," said the Riddler. "I'm ready when you are, pal!"

With a wink of his eye, the Bat-Mite vanished along with the Riddler.

CHAPTER 5

THE BIG SNEEZE!

POP! Riddler and Bat-Mite magically appeared in the Museum of Art. They stood in front of a painting titled "Funny Money".

"Finally, it's all mine!" the Riddler said. He threw his arms wide open to hug his new-found treasure.

The painting showed different kinds of coins, but each had something funny about it. The Queen was giving a thumbs up, and the unicorn and the lion on a pound coin were dancing arm in arm.

"When Batman finds out I'm robbing the museum for the second time, he'll be down in the dumps!" said the Riddler.

The Riddler looked at Bat-Mite. "Get it? Down in the *dumps*?" Riddler asked.

Bat-Mite just shrugged.

"You see," Riddler explained, "Batman thought I was going to steal the funny money at the rubbish dump! Instead, I stole the painting called 'Funny Money'!"

Suddenly, Batman soared down to the ground from his Batrope! "Guess again, Riddler!" he said.

"Batman?" the Riddler gasped in surprise. "On the police radio, you said you were going to the rubbish dump!"

"I thought you might be listening to our radio," said Batman as he landed.

"Nice work, detective," said the criminal. "But I've learned a few new tricks since the last time we met!"

The Riddler ripped the painting from the wall. A loud alarm began to ring.

"Tell me, Batman, why do sharks swim in salt water?" the Riddler cried as he fled with his prize under one arm. As he ran, he tossed a handful of green powder at Batman's face. POOF!

"Because pepper water makes them sneeze!" cackled the villain.

"Oh-oh! Looks like Riddler's having another 'sure thing'," said Bat-Mite. He was hiding behind a suit of armour. "That must be so boring for him. Let's make it fun!"

The little imp winked his eye. In the corner of the room, a large fan suddenly appeared. Its powerful blast of air blew the Riddler's own pepper cloud back at him.

The master of riddles received a face full of his own trick pepper!

"Ah-choo!" sneezed the Riddler. "What in the – ah-choo!"

With another wink, Bat-Mite's magic made a large tapestry drop from the wall. It landed on top of the sneezing Riddler, trapping him.

Under the rug, the Riddler sniffled and sneezed. He began to crawl out from under the tapestry when he bumped into something.

"I have a riddle for you, Riddler," Batman said, grabbing him by the shirt.

"What's eight feet by eight feet and has bars on the doors?" Batman asked.

"I know, I know!" squealed Bat-Mite. The little imp came skipping out from hiding, waving his hand in the air. "A jail cell!"

"So it *was* you helping the Riddler, Bat-Mite," said Batman.

"Ah-choo!" sneezed the Riddler.

"You aren't surprised, Batman?" asked Bat-Mite.

"Not really," said Batman. "Magic was the only explanation for how the Riddler switched the steel statue for the plaster one at the museum. And when there's magic involved, you're not far behind, Bat-Mite."

"I only helped the Riddler so he could give you riddles to solve," said the imp, frowning. "Didn't you have fun?"

As much as Batman wanted to be angry at the Bat-Mite, the Caped Crusader knew that the imp meant well. Still, Batman decided the little imp should go home where he could not make more trouble for the people of Gotham City.

"Yes, Bat-Mite, I had fun. Thank you," said Batman. "Just promise me you won't help anyone break the law ever again, for any reason."

"Okay, I promise," said Bat-Mite. "So, what's our next case, partner?"

"Um . . . you haven't received your medal for helping me solve this case yet!" said Batman.

"A medal?" said Bat-Mite. "For me?"

Batman removed a shiny silver tracking device from his Utility Belt.

CLICK! Batman snapped the device to the front of Bat-Mite's costume. To Bat-Mite, the silver disc looked like the biggest medal in the world.

"I award you Batman's Silver Medal for helping me capture the Riddler!" Batman said.

"Wow! I can hardly wait for all my friends back home to see this!" said Bat-Mite. He was dancing a happy little dance in mid-air and admiring his silver medal. "Would you mind if I went home to show them, Batman?"

"Not at all," Batman smiled. "I'm sure everyone will be very proud of you."

"Thanks, partner," giggled Bat-Mite.

POP! With a wink of his eye, the little imp began to disappear.

The Caped Crusader reached into his Utility Belt and grabbed a pair of Bat-Cuffs. He reached down and cuffed the Riddler, then lifted him to his feet.

"I hope that was as much fun for you as it was for me," the Dark Knight said.

"Ah-choo!" the Riddler sneezed.

Batman grinned. "Gesundheit!" he said.

Bat-Mite

REAL NAME: Unknown

OCCUPATION: Magical imp

BASE: Another dimension

HEIGHT:
About 60 cm

WEIGHT:
Unknown

EYES:
Brown

HAIR:
Unknown

Bat-Mite is a magical imp from another dimension. He uses his special powers to travel to Earth so that he can visit his favourite super hero, Batman. Bat-Mite adores the Dark Knight so much that he has created a miniature Batman costume that looks just like his idol's suit. Bat-Mite usually tries to help Batman, but most of the time the misguided imp just ends up complicating the Caped Crusader's life. He may be a magical pain, but the playful Bat-Mite means well, so Batman usually forgives his "greatest fan".

G.C.P.D. GOTHAM CITY POLICE DEPARTMENT

- Bat-Mite's superpowers come from an advanced technology in another dimension. People on Earth cannot fully understand how this technology works, so Bat-Mite's tricks seem like magic!

- Not content to wait around for Batman to find crimes to solve, Bat-Mite has often created problems just so that he can watch his favourite super hero show off his crime-fighting skills.

- Bat-Mite has teamed up with Mr Mxyzptlk, a magical imp from the Fifth Dimension, on more than one occasion. Each time, the combined efforts of Batman, Robin, and Superman were required to put an end to their magical mischief.

- Bat-Mite helped to create an organization in honour of the Last Son of Krypton. He and the other founding members idolize Superman, claiming everyone should "put your hand in the hand of the man with heat vision".

CONFIDENTIAL

 BIOGRAPHIES

Paul Kupperberg has written many books for children, like *Wishbone: The Sirian Conspiracy* and *Powerpuff Girls: Buttercup's Terrible Temper Tantrums*. He has also written over 600 comic book stories about Superman, the Justice League, Spider-Man, Hulk, the Justice Society of America, Scooby Doo, and many, many others. He has been an editor for DC Comics, *Weekly World News*, and World Wrestling Entertainment. Paul lives with his wife Robin, son Max, and dog, Spike.

From the age of 11, **Gregg Schigiel** knew that he wanted to be a cartoonist. He has worked on projects featuring the characters Batman, Spider-Man, SpongeBob SquarePants, and just about everything in between.

Lee Loughridge has been working in comics for more than 14 years. He currently lives in a tent on the beach.

GLOSSARY

complex very complicated or difficult

counterfeit something fake that has been made to look like the real thing

cowl large, loose hood

dimension place or time in space that is different from ours

imp small, naughty creature

lopsided unbalanced, with one side heavier, larger, or higher than the other

mischievous playful, annoying, or causing trouble

scheme plan or plot for doing something that is secret or dishonest

shatter break into tiny pieces

squad small group of people involved in the same activity

DISCUSSION QUESTIONS

1. Do you think Bat-Mite is a villain, or just a harmless prankster? What are your reasons?

2. Which illustration in this book is your favourite? Explain your answer.

3. Who is more to blame for Batman's troubles – the Riddler or Bat-Mite? Why?

WRITING PROMPTS

1. Write about the next time Bat-Mite turns up in Gotham City. What kinds of problems does he cause for the Dark Knight? How will Batman deal with the strange imp? You decide.

2. Rewrite your favourite chapter in this book from Bat-Mite's perspective. Why is he helping the Riddler? Why does he like Batman so much?

3. If you had Bat-Mite's magical powers, what would you do with them? Write about the adventures you would have using your new-found superpowers.

MORE NEW BATMAN™ ADVENTURES!

KILLER CROC HUNTER

TWO-FACE'S DOUBLE TAKE

ROBIN'S FIRST FLIGHT

THE PUPPET MASTER'S REVENGE

HARLEY QUINN'S SHOCKING SURPRISE